Let the Tears Fall

Gale Nemec

Let the Tears Fall

Gale Nemec

ISBN: 978-1-947608-31-3

Nemec Productions LLC
Alexandria, Virginia

DEDICATION

Amazing days passed, amazing todays, amazing tomorrows, amazing eternity
and to our imagination.

Awe - to inspire or fill with awe. Place of beauty. Respect filled with reverence. Awesome. A powerful, profound astonishment inspired by God's greatness, power, and majesty.

Let your tears fall.

This book belongs to

This book is from

Today's date

God held your hand,

As you rested on the sand.

Happy as could be,

After swimming in the sea.

God held your hand,

As you lay upon the sand,

Your left hand on your heart

Your right hand apart,

Relaxing at your side

Wide open with

nothing to hide.

After you swam

in the deep, blue green sea,

doing what you wanted to do,

and where you wanted to be.

Loving the evening

and the sound of the sea,

Smiling. . .

God looked at you,

and gently said,

"My Child. It's Your time.

Come with me"

God held your hand.

As He lifted you off the sand,

And lovingly floated you

into the air

never more to have

a worry or care.

When you turned, and looked

into Christ loving face,

You saw and felt

a magnificent new place.

A place you simply could not
describe -

It was brilliant!

It was beautiful!

It was. . . it was. . .

. . . It filled you inside.

Suddenly you looked down,

to the deep blue sea

and excitedly shouted,

"Hey, look! There!

On the beach!

That person!! That's me!"

"No," God explained,

"not anymore.

You just passed through

my fascinating door.

What you see below

is behind you now."

You looked at Him

in awe and understanding
and said,

"Oh. . .

. . .wow. . ."

God smiled.
And lifted you
higher in the air.

You flew!
You floated!
You tumbled. . .
You jumped everywhere!

Up, up, up into endless space,

then down, down, down

with sparkly fish you raced.

Dolphins, whales, and

schools of fish, too!

Through shipwrecks, cities

and reefs, who knew?!

Seeing, for the first time,
countless things
for you to see and do!

Galaxies, planets, moons,

stars, and suns!

It was absolutely crazy –

It was so much fun!

Eskimos in igloos and

deep into the woods

Shouting and playing

wherever you stood!

Meeting the people,

you always wanted to know,

Hugging your loved ones –

who'd left you below.

Your laughter rang out

and echoed through space.

Your jaw constantly dropping

at this awesome, endless place.

You clapped your hands!

You shook your head!

You knew in your heart

you'd never need

another bed.

Together you walked,

flew and swam away,

Into a brand new,
indescribable,

never-ending fulfilling day.

With colors so brilliant

You couldn't describe

They glistened! They bounced!

They brought a tear

to your eye.

Holding His great big,

comfortable hand

He led you to a new,

and unknown land.

Invisible to those

here on earth

But for you –

a brand new,

exhilarating

birth.

As you entered into

your glorious new life,

where you'd never again

have pain or strife.

You were filled with so much

wonder and awe.

That all you could say was,

"Ahhhh –

and sing

Your favorite song.

You sang it as loud
as you possibly could.
Then slower and faster
echoing through the
deep green woods.
As soft as soft
as you wanted it to be
changing its rhythm
spo-rad-i-ca-lly,
and sometimes. . .
. . .slapping your
invisible
knee!!

There was so much now

you had been shown.

Previously only guessed at

and completely unknown.

When God held your hand,

as He lifted you off the sand,

after swimming

and splashing

in the sea,

Which was Exactly

where you wanted to be.

Your passing was gentle,

from this life to the next.

It was peaceful.

It was quiet

and awesomely blessed.

Now...

. . .God and You

hold each other's hands,

your spirit is

with Him

and no longer on the sand.

Arm in arm

floating by His side,

writing, dreaming, visiting us,

loving this

forever ride

and realizing,

"God held My hand!

As I lay upon the sand,

after swimming in the sea

Happier than I could ever be.

Wwweeeeee!"

In memory. . .let your tears fall

Books, E-Books, and Audible Books
By Gale Nemec
Gale Nemec Books
Motivate. Create. Educate.

www.GaleNemecBooks.com
GaleNemecBooks@gmail.com

Little Stockey & The Miracle of Christmas
There's A Bear on A Bench
The Great Elephant Rescue
Throwing Rocks in the River
No Valentines for Trevor or Emily
Valentines for Valentines Day
Trevor and the T's
Andy's Adventurous Nightmare
A Window into Heaven
Hugs
Hugs, Two. A memory and keepsake
photo book
Benjamin Loves the Beach
Santa's Gift a drawing book for Girls
Santa's Gift a drawing book for Boys
A Wish for You
Let the Tears Fall

Bilingual: English Spanish

Hay un Oso En La Banca (Bear on A Bench)
El pequeño Stockey y el Milagro de la
Navidad (Little Stockey & the Miracle of
Christmas)

Non-Fiction

Caught in the Crosshairs of War

You Tube Channel Gale Nemec
Your Song-The Ten Commandments Song
Interact with Gale as she reads to kids.

There's a Bear on a Bench
Throwing Rocks in the river
And watch
Line! Little Stockey & the Miracle of Christmas!

PLEASE VISIT. LISTEN, LIKE AND SHARE.

Thank you for reading and buying this book.
Please rate it on Amazon, Good Reads, Google
and where you bought it with a star value or a
written review. Your review and stars will help
others to enjoy this book, too!

About the Author

Gale Nemec is an award-winning producer, actress, and voice talent. She is also a songwriter. Her most recent song *Your Song The Ten Commandment Song* , a song you can sing and dance to, is on Gale Nemec YouTube channel as well as online.

She created and produced *The Bea & the Bug* an award winning, multimedia, interactive musical show now *Adventure in Time, the Ultimate Time-Travel Series for Kids!* featuring known and not so well known, people in American history - A touring show and online series!

www.AitTvWeb.com
AitTvWeb@gmail.com

Jesus loves you

www.ingramcontent.com/pod-product-compliance
Lightning Source LLC
Chambersburg PA
CBHW041031170626
46815CB00001B/51